W9-BKE-396

– DEDICATION –

This book is dedicated to all those who have played a role in the preservation of the Scituate Lighthouse
from the day when Hingham carpenters drove the first nail to today's active Scituate Historical Society.

I would like to also dedicate this book to my wife Judy who played an important role in the creation of the story and
today inspires all who know her with her determination and courage as she recovers from a stroke.

No one writes a book alone. This story was written thanks to my parents, teachers, mentors, the giants of literature
along with suggestions from Bob, Julie and Haley Gallagher, Dave Ball, Louie Bartos and his wife Jean
and the support of residents of Cedar Point and many wonderful photographers.
Thank you all,
Richard

FAMILY LIFE
PUBLISHING

R.M. WAINWRIGHT BOOKS/FAMILY LIFE PUBLISHING
87 Rebecca Road, Scituate, MA 02066
1-800-633-1357
www.rmwainwrightbooks.com

Text Copyright (c)2013 Richard M. Wainwright
Text Editors: Julie Gallagher, Coleby Mantz and Henley Smith
Photography Editors: Linda Martin, Dave Ball, and Bob & Julie Gallagher
Layout Editor and Book Designer: Mary Sellner Orr

First Edition
All rights reserved. No part of this book may be reproduced or utilized in any form by any means,
electrical or mechanical including photocopying, recording, or by any information storage and retrieval system,
without written permission from the publisher or the Scituate Historical Society.

Printed in Singapore by Tien Wah Press.
Published in the United State of America, 2013

ISBN: 978-0-9619566-9-1

– THE TALE OF –
The Scituate Lightkeeper's Daughter

To_____

May every day in your life be a treasure.

Best Wishes,

Richard M. Wainwright

From_____

– CHAPTER I –

Visitors to Front Street in Scituate, Massachusetts can shop and, at the same time, keep in view the lovely harbor and prominent lighthouse. As the oldest complete lighthouse in the United States, its history has fascinated generations.

The peninsula enclosing the northern side of Scituate Harbor is known as Cedar Point whose nightly flashing jewel is its lighthouse. This light beckons and welcomes neighbors from nearby towns, travelers from across the United States and tourists from around the world. In front of the lighthouse is a parking lot where harborside benches invite onlookers to sit and stay for awhile.

Residents and visitors can be seen on Cedar Point each day and evening walking with friends, with their dogs or jogging as bicyclers pass by. Some people come to this special place to get married in front of the lighthouse; others bring their antique cars for weekly reunions; and during the year hundreds come to watch sailing regattas, colorful parades, a flying Santa or simply to find some tranquil moments while looking seaward at the great Atlantic or the beautiful sailboats moored in Scituate Harbor's calm waters.

The lighthouse has stood on the tip of Cedar Point peninsula since 1811. In that year, three men from the nearby town of Hingham built the 25-foot-tall stone tower, a one-and-a-half-story Keeper's House, its oil vault and a well for thirty-two hundred dollars. Its lamps were first lit on September 19th of the same year and were visible six miles to sea.

Bob and Julie Gallagher, and their daughter Haley, were the 13th official Keepers of Scituate Light. Haley Gallagher, a charming, outgoing pretty thirteen year old young lady, often walked around "The Point" visiting and chatting with neighbors. She was smart, enjoyed school, and even though she was barely a teenager Haley told her friends that she and her parents were putting money aside hoping one day she could go to college.

Five days a year, the Gallaghers hosted an Open House to show guests the lighthouse's living quarters, relate Scituate Light's fascinating history and lead them up the tower to the light and its 360-degree view of the open sea to the east and Scituate's snug harbor to the west.

Haley enjoyed the company of many friends but on Open House days, along with her parents, she was on duty welcoming visitors and relating the fascinating history of Scituate Light. The family explained old pictures and showed artifacts. They described the lives of early Keepers and the conditions they faced and how today's Scituate Lighthouse functions along with the responsibilities of its Keeper. Often there were lines of people waiting to take the tour to the tower.

Residents of this lovely seaside community and visitors to Cedar Point did not realize that the lighthouse still had a tale to tell. During a late summer Open House a strange visitor would add to the history of Scituate Light and change Haley's life forever.

One Saturday at the end of August unusual weather blanketed the town of Scituate. Dawn never seemed to arrive. It was first hidden by a dense haze which in turn was overwhelmed by a thick wet fog that rolled in from the sea. The day was as dark as some nights. The pea soup fog was the most bizarre weather ever experienced during an Open House.

Cars drove very, very slowly down Lighthouse Road toward the parking lot. No one could see more than a few feet in front of them. It was an eerie world. Even at water's edge Scituate's beautiful harbor could not be seen, nor its lighthouse. Nevertheless by 1:00 PM a crowd in jackets and raincoats stood quietly in line waiting their turn to enter the lighthouse and the narrow sparsely lit wooden corridor which led to the light tower.

Haley was at her post near the entrance door greeting each visitor. Everyone mentioned the strange weather. The afternoon passed quickly and eventually the line grew short.

Sterling, Haley's cat, had a great afternoon. He loved attention and had received several hours of caresses and pats. As each visitor stepped into the house Sterling rubbed his back against willing legs. The tactic worked well until a young boy stepped across the threshold. Sterling's green eyes became fearful, the fur on the back of his fluffy gray neck stood straight up as he bolted for Haley's room in search of a hiding spot under her bed. The cat trembled as it stared through Haley's open door.

Haley had noticed a thin boy at the very end of the line. He was wearing a white shirt with a wide open collar and had a black scarf around his neck. His baggy white pants hung a few inches below his knees, and much to Haley's surprise, he was barefoot.

The people in front of him stopped and chatted with Haley before they began climbing the stairs to the lighthouse tower. A few had noticed the boy and his shaggy brown hair which was rumpled like an unmade bed. His brown eyes contrasted with his colorless complexion. The people in line who had observed the strangely dressed small boy thought he could be between the age of ten and thirteen. It was hard to even guess.

One man in line was an historian and believed the clothes the boy was wearing were similar to what seamen wore a long time ago. The gentleman thought maybe the boy was a member of the lighthouse staff and was wearing sea faring period clothes for the day. Several people laughingly whispered that the lad was probably going to a costume party. No one was right.

One by one each person or family stopped and spoke with Haley before moving on. Often she would tell the story of the first Light Keeper, Simeon Bates, and his wife Rachel, who lived in the small Keeper's house with nine of their eleven children beginning in December of 1811. Haley would always relate the heroic deeds of two of the Bates' daughters, eighteen-year-old Abigail and twenty-year-old Rebecca.

In June 1814, two British warships, the *Bulwark* and *Nymph,* had terrorized Scituate destroying vital supplies that were loaded on barges in the harbor. The townspeople of Scituate, in response to the attack, formed a two hundred and fifty man militia.

Early one morning in September that year, Abigail and Rebecca were alone at the lighthouse. Looking seaward they spotted a British warship anchoring just outside the harbor. They were deathly afraid the troops on board would soon come ashore in long boats. The young women grabbed their musical instruments, a fife and drum, and began playing loudly. They were good musicians and their music fooled the British Captain into believing that the Scituate militia was forming. The British sailed away without sending in their marines. Abigail's and Rebecca's fame spread and they were acclaimed Scituate's "Lighthouse Army of Two."

While Haley shared the story of the Bates sisters, the young boy listened ten paces behind the last family. When no one else was in sight he walked forward and stood alone in front of Haley. He was a couple of inches shorter than she.

Haley greeted him with her perpetual smile as she wondered why he was so peculiarly dressed. She sensed there was something very different about this boy. His colorless complexion made Haley wonder if he was ill, yet at the same time, she immediately felt that an inexplicable aura surrounded him, almost like the fog outside. Of course, she could not see anything specific. It was just a strong feeling she had.

The boy didn't smile but nodded his head acknowledging her words of welcome.

Haley asked the boy his name trying not to stare at his strange clothes or at his ashen face which looked young and old at the same time. He did not scare her but for some reason she began to feel slightly dizzy and a little nauseous.

In a hoarse whisper the boy spoke, "I will tell thee. Walter Eldridge is my name. My family came to Scituate in a wagon a long time ago. I never saw your lighthouse from the land. Years later I saw your lighthouse from the sea – 'tis not quite the same today!"

Haley wondered. *What did this boy mean? "A long time ago? Not the same today?" How could that be? He could not be much older than I am.*

Walter spoke again. "Pray tell me what happened when the USS Frigate *Chesapeake* and the British warship HMS *Shannon* fought not far from this lighthouse in 1813?"

Haley paused almost speechless. Although she knew the history of the naval battle, few adults asked about the famous engagement – never mind a child about her age who spoke funny.

"Well, you may know," she began, "the USS *Chesapeake* was a 38-gun three-masted heavy frigate of the United States Navy. She was built and launched from Portsmouth, Virginia on December 2nd, 1802.

"The *Chesapeake* began her career during the war with France in combat at the First Barbary Coast War. On the 22nd of June in 1807 she was fired upon and captured by the HMS *Leopard* of the Royal Navy for refusing to comply with a search for deserters. Some American sailors were taken by the British. The Chesapeake-Leopard Affair angered the American people. Our government passed the Embargo Act of 1807 against England and this was one of the factors that led President James Madison and the Congress to declare war against England in 1812."

Walter nodded. "Aye, 'tis the truth you say – pray go on."

Haley hesitated and then continued, "Early in the war the *Chesapeake* made one patrol and captured five British merchant ships." For the first time, Walter slightly smiled but didn't say anything.

Haley paused, then spoke, "On the morning of June 1st 1813, the *Chesapeake* sailed from Boston Harbor looking for a British warship. By six in the evening she was not far from this lighthouse. Near the cliffs of Scituate the USS *Chesapeake* engaged the HMS *Shannon* which had been blockading Boston Harbor."

Walter looked deadly serious, "Aye she did. 'Twas my thirteenth birthday," he murmured. Haley stopped. She could not have heard correctly.

Haley went on. "It was a horrible but short battle. The two ships were about the same size but the crew on the HMS *Shannon* was very well trained and had more experience. Almost simultaneously the ships fired their cannons and the USS *Chesapeake* lost its masts and steerage.

"The HMS *Shannon's* first volley killed many of the USS *Chesapeake's* sailors. Its surviving crew fought valiantly as the *Shannon's* sailors boarded the U.S. ship. In all, sixty-one American sailors died. Some fell overboard and were lost at sea. As I said, it was all over in less than a quarter of an hour."

Walter's eyes had not left Haley's lips as she spoke. In an obviously sad voice, Walter spoke, "Aye, it was a slaughter. Most of the powder monkeys died in the first volley. Pray tell me the fate of good Captain Lawrence?"

Haley was perplexed thinking that Walter seemed to know as much as she did about the battle but she answered his question.

"Captain Lawrence was mortally wounded early in the battle. As he was being taken below to his cabin he told his sailors, 'Don't give up the ship!' "

Walter's head dropped to his chest as he muttered, "I never ken." He raised his head with a look of sad understanding.

"Thank you, lass. The first time I went to sea, I met a sailor who had sailed the seven seas. He was known as Old Simon and he became my best friend and mentor. Sadly, that was to be his last voyage. Before he died Old Simon gave me his worldly belongings. I lost them but I know where they are and I would like to give them to you. Will thou accept a wee gift?"

Haley was thinking of some of the boy's words... *My family came to Scituate a long time ago... Powder Monkeys... I went to sea... Lost something but I know where it is...*" The boy had confused Haley. She wanted to ask him many questions but she simply stammered politely, "Yes – thank you."

For the first time Walter smiled broadly. "Haley," he began, "in this neighborhood you will find another *Walter*. Follow him home, look beneath his 360-degree view and you will find a wee treasure. Now I must go. Good-bye to you."

Haley stood speechless, frozen to the spot, and managed only a weak smile. Without another word, the boy turned and stepped out the door into the thick fog.

The queasy feeling in Haley's stomach and lightheaded feeling passed soon after the stranger, Walter Eldridge, departed. She felt as if she had just woken up from a restless sleep. Haley was upset with herself for not having the courage to ask the boy some questions. She decided to go after him to get answers.

Haley stepped outside. Massive dark black clouds that had laid above the fog were being blown north. The fog began to lift. Haley could see about fifty feet down her driveway but Walter Eldridge was nowhere in sight. She then ran into the parking lot. Haley saw the shapes of a few adults but no young boy. She hesitated. In that instant, like magic, the fog completely disappeared.

Haley rushed to look down Lighthouse Road, and seeing no one, ran to the other side of the parking lot to stare down Rebecca Road. She saw no one. Slowly, she turned back toward the lighthouse.

Haley stopped beside the small group of people who had visited the lighthouse and were still chatting in the parking lot. They were facing the lighthouse and some were taking pictures. She thought they must have seen the boy and she decided to ask them.

Much to her surprise, no one had seen a young boy dressed in a white shirt and pants coming from the direction of the lighthouse. Although they had all been looking toward the fog-enshrouded building the whole time they had not seen anyone. Of course, they said it had been very foggy until just a few minutes ago.

Haley slowly retraced her steps to the lighthouse and went right to her room. She lay down on her bed. Sterling, who had been curled up in a ball hiding under her bed, jumped up to join her. Haley cuddled him. Sterling purred loudly. As Haley petted her cat she wondered if she should tell her parents about the strange young visitor. How could he have disappeared so fast? Could she have just imagined or dreamt meeting the boy?

15

All through the evening, even as she prepared for sleep, "Walter Eldridge" remained in her mind. After turning out the lights, Haley always looked out her window. The night was cloudless, a harvest moon was rising and boats gently rocked in the harbor. It was a serene and comforting scene which gave her a peaceful feeling that someday her questions would be answered.

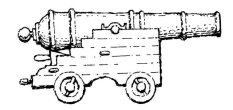

– CHAPTER II –

Cries of squabbling gulls fighting over a fish carcass awakened Haley. It was Sunday morning so she smiled to herself knowing there was no rush to get up. Yet, almost immediately, her thoughts returned to the previous day and all the visitors that had come to tour the lighthouse.

Most of the faces were a blur, but the one that remained clearly in her memory was of a boy, possibly close to her age, dressed in white with a presence Haley knew she would never forget.

Haley dressed, thinking about the strange meeting, and decided that she would not mention it to her parents at breakfast. Later in the morning she would pay a visit to some of her neighbors and find out if anyone knew of someone named Walter who might be living in the neighborhood. Haley knew it was a crazy idea and she laughed at herself. Still, it would be fun to see her friends before returning for the second day of the Open House weekend, which would again begin at 1:00 PM.

By eleven in the morning, unlike the previous day, the sun was shining brightly and Haley left the lighthouse. She immediately spotted JP's Hotdog Express in the lighthouse parking lot. Joe Spinzola and Paula Polaski were setting up their tent, table and mobile kitchen getting ready for customers.

Spotting Haley as she crossed the road, Joe and Paula welcomed her with smiles and greetings.

"Hi, Guys! How were sales yesterday in the fog? Did many people find you?" Haley asked.

"Your visitors found us all right," Joe answered, "and I think the fog made everyone hungry. By the time the sun came out we had sold out of our half pound cheeseburgers and our pulled pork barbecue sandwiches. We had a great day. Thanks."

Haley spoke, "I'm glad it turned out to be a busy day for JP's. By the way, I bet you know almost everyone who lives on Cedar Point. Do you know of anyone named Walter who might live in any of the houses on Lighthouse Road or Rebecca Road?"

Joe and Paula thought for a minute and then they shook their heads. "Of course," said Joe, "If you are including one with four legs, then Carol Ann and Tony have an English Bulldog named Walter." They all chuckled.

Even as she was laughing Haley thought of the strange boy's cryptic words… *In this neighborhood you will find another Walter. Follow him home, look beneath his 360-degree view and you will find a wee treasure.*

Could he have meant a dog? Haley wondered. She thought of Walter the dog knowing he was never out alone. Haley told Joe and Paula she hoped they would have another busy day and turned toward Lighthouse Road.

Haley didn't see anyone until she got to Tony and Carol Ann's house. She paused, wondering if anyone was home. Just at that moment Carol Ann opened the front door to take her English Bulldog, Walter, out for a walk. She invited Haley to sit for a minute. They chatted briefly on the porch steps. A few minutes later Bridget and Ed, next door neighbors, wandered over with their dog, Jack, and joined in the conversation.

Eventually Haley asked if Walter had a favorite spot in his house or his yard. Carol Ann laughed telling Haley that Walter had many favorite spots in the neighborhood. In the house Walter visited most of their rooms daily but he especially liked lying in front of the sliding glass door which looked out to Scituate Harbor.

Haley asked the group if they knew of anyone named Walter who lived nearby. Almost in unison, they shook their heads. Haley gave the friendly English Bulldog one more pat before saying goodbye. To herself she said, *Four-legged Walter doesn't make any sense!*

Haley visited the Jacobs, Winters, and Caspersens and finally the home of the Hoovers. She asked everyone if they knew anyone named Walter that lived in the neighborhood or nearby. No one knew of a two-legged Walter.

It was time for Haley to head back to the lighthouse and take her place with her parents to greet the Sunday visitors. It had been nice to chat with her neighbors but now she felt a little silly. She returned to her idea that yesterday's encounter was simply a figment of her imagination yet her memory of the strangely dressed boy seemed so real.

By the time Haley returned and combed her hair there was a line of people waiting to take a tour of the lighthouse. She opened the front door to let them in. Haley again answered questions and related the history of the lighthouse to visitors waiting to climb the stairs to the tower. It was a busy afternoon.

There were a number of children with their parents but on this day a young boy dressed in white did not make an appearance. Haley wasn't surprised. Even though she could remember every word he spoke, the boy named Walter Eldridge must have been just an exceptionally vivid daydream.

The remaining seven days of summer vacation passed quickly for Haley. She had much to do getting ready to return to Gates Intermediate Middle School, yet hardly an hour went by that she didn't think of the mysterious stranger who had come to Scituate Lighthouse.

School opened the following Monday. Haley tried to put memories of the last Open House Weekend behind her. However, by Wednesday, thoughts of Walter Eldridge came rushing back when her teacher, Mrs. Hart, asked the students to use their imagination and write a fictional story about something that might have happened during the summer in Scituate. Haley silently laughed to herself thinking she could write about her dream boy, Walter Eldridge, and his fanciful gift.

Friday after school she saw her friend Morgan. They didn't see much of each other during the week as they were in different schools. On this Friday, Morgan had to deliver Girl Scout goodies to people around "The Point." Haley offered to help. While going house to house they talked about a lot of things including school, music and movies and finally ended up chatting on the jetty beside the lighthouse.

Morgan brought up the subject of the previous Saturday's abnormal pea soup foggy weather. "Haley, you won't believe this but I had a really weird experience that day. I read a book for a couple of hours and then decided, even if I could only see a few feet in front of me, I needed some fresh air. Slowly I biked to Cedar Point. I planned to spend time with you after your open house was over. Very carefully I followed the path to the lighthouse tower and found a boulder close to where we are sitting now. I knew you were inside the lighthouse talking with visitors.

"I could barely see the calm ocean even though it was only a few feet below me. I felt like I was wrapped in a warm blanket of mist. It gave me a relaxed and peaceful feeling. I sat with my arms around my knees and stared out toward the sea enjoying the quiet. Except for the occasional muted sound of a car leaving the parking lot there was only a deep silence. I sat there for about ten minutes. It was then I thought I heard creaking noises an old wooden boat would make along with faint unintelligible voices floating through the thick mist. I tried to see through the fog. I couldn't at first but then the fog thinned a little.

"For only a moment I saw a large floating object just beyond the end of the jetty. It disappeared in the blink of an eye. As I stared in the same direction the thickness of the fog kept changing. Once more a hole in the fog gave me a good look at what seemed to be a large three-masted ship. It was only for a few seconds but I am sure that I saw it. It reminded me of 'Old Ironsides,' the USS *Constitution* in Boston.

"When I returned home I went on my computer and researched sailing ships shaped like the one I saw. This probably sounds crazy but the ship I saw must have been built about the same time as 'Old Ironsides' which was launched in 1797. As you know, the fog eventually lifted so I went back and searched the sea beyond the jetty and of course there wasn't even a lobster boat in sight. I felt confused and decided to go home to continue reading but it was hard to concentrate. Maybe it was an optical illusion or I need glasses or as they say in Australia I have 'Gone round the bend.' "

Haley laughed. "Morgan, you have eyes like a hawk. I don't think you need glasses and you haven't 'Gone round the bend.' Yes, it was a weird day. I had a strange experience that day too. I will tell you about it next week but now I must get home for dinner and start on a writing assignment for school."

That evening, before Haley started her assignment, she decided to research the words "Powder Monkeys" which had been like a pesky fly in her mind. On her computer she found many references. She went to Wikipedia first and began to read…

> "**Powder monkeys** were a part of warships' crews during the **Age of Sail** that carried bags of gunpowder from the **powder magazine** in the ship's hold to the gun crews. Powder monkeys were usually boys or young teens selected for the job for their speed and height – they were short and would be hidden behind the ship's gunwale, keeping them from being shot by enemy ships' sharp shooters… in close quarter battles, they were often some of the first casualties… The use of the term 'powder monkey' in English dates to the late 17th century."

Haley reread the paragraph and stared at the picture of the powder monkey. The young boy in the picture had on a white sailor's shirt with a black scarf and loose fitting pants that fell below his knees. The outfit was identical to the clothes worn by the strange visitor who called himself Walter Eldridge. Haley relived their meeting several times before she could concentrate enough to begin her writing assignment.

When finished for the night, Haley decided next weekend she would continue walking around Cedar Point and ask other neighbors and friends if they knew of anyone named Walter.

The following Saturday was bright and sunny yet quite cool with autumn in the air. As Haley crossed the lighthouse parking lot she spotted Cedar Point's friendly postman, Mark Walkins, getting out of his delivery truck. Haley quickly went over to say "hi" thinking he might just have the answer she was looking for. Did he know of anyone named Walter that lived on his route?

Mark thought a moment, "Maybe fifteen years ago there was a Walter Smith who lived on Rebecca Road for a short time but I can't think of anyone else. Sorry, Haley."

Haley thanked Mr. Walkins and headed for Dave and Joanne Ball's house. Dave had lived in Scituate all his life and had been the president of the Scituate Historical Society for many years. If anyone would know of someone named Walter living in the neighborhood it would be Mr. Ball.

Haley also knew that even if Mr. Ball didn't know of anyone, he always had fascinating tales to tell, usually something interesting about the history of Scituate. Maybe he would say something that she could include in the story she was writing for school. After knocking on the front door Haley asked Mrs. Ball if she could have a few moments of their time. Mrs. Ball invited Haley inside and Mr. Ball joined them. They all sat down in the living room. Haley told them about her writing assignment and that her story was going to be about a young boy who visited the Lighthouse and a lost treasure. She did not give any further details about Walter Eldridge's appearance.

"Do you know of anyone named Walter in this neighborhood?" Haley asked. She expected to simply hear another "No."

"Well," Dave began, "I can't think of anyone that has lived on Cedar Point in recent years but if you go way back in history there was a Quaker family that lived in Scituate around 1808 by the name of Eldridge. They had four children including a young son named Walter who, according to old letters, went to sea at age eleven as a powder monkey. I don't know what happened to him but I do remember reading that a year or so after the War of 1812 began, the family left town."

Haley was stunned and barely able to speak. She tried to hide her surprise by telling Mr. Ball that maybe she could use his information in her story.

Was it possible that "Walter" was the spirit of a boy who lost his life in the terrible battle between the USS *Chesapeake* and the HMS *Shannon* in 1813?

Her head spinning, Haley barely remembered to thank the Balls. In a daze, Haley crossed the street to visit the Martin Family. Mrs. Martin was never too busy to share a few moments. Linda Martin listened to Haley's ideas for her story. She did not know of anyone living in the neighborhood named Walter but said she would ask her husband Peter when he returned from work.

Almost in a trance Haley continued up the street stopping to speak with Betty and John Kincaid, Judy and Tom Knightly, Kathy and Brian Loftus, and Betty and Bob McCarron. All offered ideas for her story but no one knew of someone named Walter presently or recently living in a house on Cedar Point.

Haley's last stop would be the Wainwrights. She hoped Judy was home. Haley climbed the porch stairs and rapped on the front door. Judy greeted her saying, "Hi, Haley! You are just in time to test my chocolate chip cookies fresh out of the oven."

Haley made herself comfortable in a chair in front of the large picture windows that spanned the back of the elevated first floor. Haley looked down and over the seawall which was only twelve feet from the house. The tide was almost fully out. It would return in six hours to lap the seawall if the ocean was calm; or if rough, hammer it hard causing heavy spray to fly over the house.

The smell of warm pastries arrived before the tray of cookies and milk. Judy sat down next to Haley and gazed out her window telling Haley that she never got tired of looking at the ever-changing view of sea and sky.

"Haley, did you see the picture of the ship by our front door that looks like it could be only a few feet from these windows?"

Haley nodded.

"It is still hard for me to imagine," Judy continued, "that on March 16th, 1956, less than 200 feet from where we are sitting, a 7,000 ton, four-hundred and forty-one foot Italian freighter was driven onto those rocks by a surprise blizzard. The name of the ship was the *Etrusco*. The rescue of its crew truly is an amazing Cedar Point story of heroism by people who lived here on 'The Point' as well as in the town.

"It was a long, bitter cold snowy night for the men on the ship and those on the shore planning the rescue. By early the next morning, thanks to a rigged breeches buoy from ship to shore, all thirty members of the crew were rescued. Our fire department, town officials and the Coast Guard, along with neighbors like Lina Russo, would never be forgotten by the seamen whose lives they saved that day.

"I think you would enjoy reading the *Etrusco's* story since it happened so close to your lighthouse home."

Haley thought so too. She was about to explain the reason for her visit but at that moment there was a loud squawking from a gull on the seawall.

"That's Walter," announced Judy. "I guess he wants his lunch." Without another word Judy went to her refrigerator, got out a piece of bread and a few pieces of bluefish she had caught the previous day. Judy told Haley to watch through the window as she went outside and down the porch steps to greet Walter who was waiting patiently at his favorite place on the seawall.

Haley was surprised and mesmerized watching Judy begin speaking to a herring gull with brown freckles dotting its white neck. It had a gray back and black tail feathers with four white spots. Judy sat down on the seawall. The gull watched from a respectful distance. When food appeared in Judy's hand "Walter" quickstepped up to her and snatched the morsels from her fingers.

Unafraid, the sea bird remained in front of Judy waiting for each item on the menu to appear. Snatch, gulp and a piece of fish quickly disappeared down the gull's throat. Judy looked up at Haley who was watching through the living room window. They both smiled.

Finally, Judy's scraps of food were all gone. The gull flew away. Judy beckoned Haley to come outside and join her on the seawall.

"What do you think of our friend, Walter?" she asked Haley.

Haley wondered what to say first. "Walter?" Haley caught her breath. "Does Walter come here every day?" Haley asked.

Judy told Haley how Walter had entered Dick and Judy's lives two years ago one morning landing on the railing of their second floor deck overlooking the ocean. Judy at first just talked to the gull and put out a few Cheerios® on the flat railing for him to gobble up. Judy and Dick decided to call the herring gull Walter and from then on that became his name. Now he would come when called and although he was very wild, in time, Walter trusted Judy to feed him from her hand.

"Walter usually visits at least once a day," Judy replied. "Sometimes he will arrive squawking loudly indicating that he would like breakfast, lunch or dinner." Judy smiled as she pointed out a large boulder surrounded by water about one hundred and fifty feet from shore covered with seaweed and only visible at low tide. Sitting on the boulder was a herring gull.

"That's Walter and that's his favorite rock," Judy explained. "He often goes there after he eats. Watch him as he slowly turns taking in his 360-degree view to be sure he is safe. The tide is coming in now and in an hour that boulder will be completely under water."

Though Judy continued to talk, Haley was wrapped up in her own thoughts... *In this neighborhood you will find another Walter. Follow him home, look beneath his 360-degree view and you will find a wee treasure...* "Is there always deep water around the rock?" Haley asked.

No," Judy replied. "At dead low tide the water around Walter's perch is less then six inches deep and it stays that way for about a half hour during the tide change. It's possible to get to Walter's rock. Occasionally a few people risk going out that far to collect periwinkles and blue mussels but it is a dangerous trip due to the very slippery seaweed and kelp, which cover the rocks – a fall could mean a serious injury."

With doubt in her voice, Haley asked Judy, "Could you go out to Walter's resting place with me at low tide?"

"Do you want to collect periwinkles and blue mussels?" Judy replied. "We could find them a lot closer to shore and I've got just the bucket to put them in."

"No," Haley said with a grin. "I don't want to collect seafood. I need to get to Walter's Rock. I must go there even if you think I am crazy. How about next Saturday?"

Judy hesitated and then smiled, "We will have to be extremely careful and go very slowly, watch the tide closely and not stay there very long. Yes, I will go with you. It doesn't matter what your reason is. I promise I won't call you crazy."

– CHAPTER III –

The following Saturday morning Haley arrived at Judy's front door at 10:00 AM, which was two hours before dead low tide. Judy was ready but asked Haley to sit down, have a glass of milk and a chocolate chip cookie or two and explain the purpose of today's mission to Walter's Rock.

Haley had been thinking a lot about what she would tell Judy and decided to simply tell her exactly what she had experienced several weeks ago during Open House Weekend at the Lighthouse. After a sip of milk and a bite of a cookie, Haley began relating her tale about meeting the boy, Walter. Judy listened intently not saying a word or changing her expression until Haley had finished. "Judy, do you think this meeting could have really happened? For awhile I could not figure out if it was real or a daydream. Then, when I came here last week and met Walter, the herring gull, everything started to make sense."

Judy smiled, "Well, you're not crazy. I learned a long time ago that no one can ever assume things are impossible. Life is full of unknowns and it will always be that way – for everyone. Why do accidents happen to some people while others win the lottery? No one can answer those and many other questions. We just have to accept it as part of the mystery of life.

"We can at least try to find out whether your strange experience happened or was simply a daydream. We can dig around *my Walter's* rock hoping that it is the correct interpretation of *your Walter's* clues. Maybe we will find something – maybe we won't. It's a great day – warm, sunny and the tide is almost out so let's go on a treasure hunt!"

Judy toted a sturdy pitchfork while Haley carried a clam rake and together they held a blue bucket. They slowly made their way across the seaweed-covered rocks, around tide pools and periwinkle-covered stones. It took them over ten minutes taking one careful step after another to reach the boulder where Judy's *Walter* often perched after taking food from her on the seawall.

Judy looked at the tide pool surrounding the big boulder. Big and small rocks and small sandy spots could be easily seen through the clear, still water which was about six or seven inches deep. Judy observed, "The tide will turn soon. We have about forty-five minutes before the returning tide reaches this area. Let's pick up and dig out all the small rocks first and then we will try to see if we have any luck with the big ones." Haley nodded realizing this wasn't going to be easy.

For twenty minutes they bent down, almost in unison, reaching into the water picking up and tossing aside every rock that was not stuck in the gritty sand or in the mud wedged between other rocks. Then the really hard work began.

Haley, with clam rake, was able to loosen obstinate rocks the size of baseballs and Judy, using her big pitchfork, began tackling the football-sized stones that were half buried in the sand.

They stirred up the sand while removing stones and startled little green crabs that scurried away along with slow moving starfish. It was back-breaking work. Twenty minutes flew by. They were both getting tired and beginning to think the same thing – that their efforts were probably a waste of time.

Digging, pushing and pulling, the team dug out or moved several large stones. Judy pointed at the area they had just uncovered. There appeared to be a small piece of dirty tan cloth sticking out from under a half exposed large rock.

Judy and Haley looked at the big rock, then at each other and then at the ocean that had begun its inward journey. It would not be long before the incoming tide would force them to leave. Water in the tide pool was just below their knees. Without another word and with renewed energy, they tackled the basketball-sized stone. Judy slowly worked her large pitchfork under the rock that lay on the visible piece of cloth. She hoped that the unseen size of the stone below the sand was not as big as its top. If it was, she thought they probably wouldn't be able to move it.

Seconds later Judy thought luck might be with them as the pitchfork moved easier below the big stone. Maybe it had a flat bottom. There seemed to be a hollow spot beneath it. Judy placed a stone beneath the pitchfork for more leverage and pushed the handle down to see if she could move the boulder. It moved but not much.

The sea was coming in fast and the water in the hole was now almost two feet deep. Judy told Haley this was it. She would try to raise the stone one more time while Haley reached down and pulled on the sea-weed covered bag.

Both got ready. Judy counted to three before pushing the pitchfork handle down with all her strength. The stone rose again and Haley reached down in the water grabbing the cloth pulling the remainder of the bag out from beneath the stone. Judy let the rock fall back into place.

Haley sighed as she dropped it in their pail. "It's just an old, sandy canvas bag covered with seaweed."

Judy looked surprised and caught her breath exclaiming, "It's not just any bag – it looks to me to be a tarred ditty bag! If it is as old as I think it might be, then it is extraordinary that the tar was able to preserve it and prevent the cloth from disintegrating."

"What's a ditty bag?" Haley questioned.

Judy didn't answer as she worked the pitchfork out from under the big stone. She was exhausted from the bending, lifting and prying and knew Haley was too. She wanted to sit down and rest but saw that the tide was moving in fast.

"When we get settled back in the house," Judy replied breathlessly, "I'll tell you what I know of sailors' ditty bags but now we must move quickly before the tide catches us! Right now we do not have a second to waste."

Haley grabbed the clam rake in one hand and the bucket in the other. It was heavy. Carefully, they began the slow, torturous route back to the safety of the shore.

The best they could do was one deliberate step at a time over and around the slippery rocks, stepping just fast enough to keep ahead of the incoming ocean.

– CHAPTER IV –

It took Judy and Haley a half hour to get back to the shore to Judy's house. They were very tired. Although the treasure hunting duo was eager to examine the tarred bag, Judy suggested they put the tools away, let the bag dry out a bit, pull off most of the attached seaweed, wash up and sit down with a cold drink.

While Haley washed up, Judy put the bag in the kitchen sink rinsing the sand from the outside of the bag and removing most of the seaweed.

After filling two glasses with water and getting out snacks she returned to the sink and brought the bag to the kitchen counter, sat down and waited for Haley.

When Haley returned she could not take her eyes off the bag as she took a sip of water. Judy spoke, "Before we open the bag let me tell you what I know about sailors' ditty bags," and she picked it up.

"My father was in the Navy during World War II and he loved the sea. He often took me fishing and I came to feel the same way about the ocean. I began reading the history of famous sea voyages, ships and the lives of sailors. Ditty bags go back a long way and have been mentioned in naval literature as early as 1570. They were small hand-sewn sailcloth bags used by sailors to keep small tools, sewing equipment and personal articles.

"Ditty bags usually hung from a hook or peg next to the sailor's bunk in the forecastle at the bow of the ship where they slept and lived during their long voyages. This ditty bag is very unusual as it has been tarred to waterproof it and preserve it. It appears that someone a long time ago thought this ditty bag might end up in the sea. A seaman who made the bag covered it with tar so the sea did not destroy it. An average seaman could make this type of bag. It was one of their practical tasks as they learned to work canvas, 'palm and needle' they used to say. When we open it, the bag will probably have a seven inch mouth which is closed by that tangled hemp cord. When we untangle it you will see that each cord of the lanyard legs goes through beautiful six to eight worked-in eyelets. If this is a real ditty bag it could be two hundred years old!"

Judy handed the bag to Haley so she could see the fine workmanship of the hand sewn eyelets. "Today's canvas bags use metal grommets so this isn't any bag that fell out of a boat recently."

Judy continued holding up the bag. "See, it has a single seam and the bag is over 14 inches long with a roundish base. I can feel something in it but it could be just sand and mud.

"Do you think it is time to see if there is anything inside your ditty bag? It's your treasure! Somewhere in that ball of tarred hemp may be a Turks head knot which allows one to pull rope through the eyelets closing the bag. See if you can loosen a few of the strong strands. Maybe this nail will help. I will hold the tangled knot."

Haley took the nail trying to work it into the tangled cord. Time and seawater had bonded the tarred cord so tightly that it was hard to see separate strands. Finally, Haley was able to push the nail point through and expand the hole. Haley passed the nail to Judy and held the mass of rope as Judy tried to loosen and separate the intertwined cord.

Taking turns, it took Haley and Judy about thirty minutes of patient work to separate the tangled knots. Then they carefully worked to open the mouth of the bag. The first thing they saw was just a bit of sand. The bag had protected the contents well.

Haley reached in the bag and removed an object that was partially covered with calcium from tiny shells that had grown on it. They took it over to the sink, and with fresh water, carefully cleaned it. Soon it became obvious that it was a short-bladed pointless knife with a knotted rope handle that had been blackened with tar.

"That is definitely an old knife," Judy exclaimed. "See how the end has been rounded. This was a safety precaution so when sailors were aloft, if they dropped the knife, it would not fall to the deck possibly injuring or killing someone. The attached lanyard was either tied around sailors' necks or to their belt.

"According to naval history I have read, sea captains often made sure that the knives their sailors carried had blunt ends to insure that when arguments arose, mariners could not kill each other in a fight. This knife cut canvas just fine and the tar on the rope handle made sure that it would not easily slip from the sailor's hand. All that tar also helped preserve it for us. Let's see what else is in the ditty bag."

The next item that Haley found was a smaller tarred packet. Inside they found a thin four-inch rusty metal rod with a hook on one end and another half loop on the other end. "What could this be?" Haley asked.

"My guess," replied Judy, "Is that it is a wrought iron bench hook – a sail maker's third hand. It held the cloth or seam so the sail maker could push the needle through the canvas."

Haley found another small bound packet in the ditty bag. After slowly opening it she found that it contained five rusty needles with three distinct edges.

"Those three edges define a sailor's needle," Judy commented. "They are certainly old."

"Is there anything else in the ditty bag?"

Haley reached in, felt around and exclaimed, "There is one more packet!"

The final tarred packet was about five inches square and two inches deep.

"What do you think is in the packet?" Judy asked Haley.

"More tools for sailmaking I guess," she replied. Haley and Judy's four hands carefully loosened

the folds of the waterproof packet. When the last fold was laid back, Haley and Judy stared at a small well-preserved coin pouch sailors carried.

"You open it Haley – it is your gift from Walter Eldridge!" Judy smiled as she spoke.

Haley gently picked up the pouch. Judy was thinking that if it was a coin pouch it probably hadn't been opened for well over a hundred years. She anxiously watched as Haley struggled a few moments until it opened. As Haley turned it upside down, coins began to fall onto the counter.

Haley and Judy just looked at each other. They couldn't believe the pile of coins in front of them. Could it be that Haley's unbelievable experience really happened?

They stared at the many copper, silver and bright gold coins. Judy got up from the counter to get a magnifying glass so they could examine them better.

The tarred bag had preserved the coins well. Judy and Haley could easily read most inscriptions. There were many copper coins including English half pennies: a 1754 King George II, two King George III 1768 and 1799 and a Duke of Lancaster 1794 with a lion on a shield. They found copper coins from Russia including a beautiful 1792 five kopek coin, a 1760 Swedish Ore and a 1792 5 sols coin from France.

Amongst the silver coins were Spanish Reales dated 1721, 1783 and 1811; a 1795 Dutch two Stuiver; a 1766 200 Reis coin from Portugal; and 5 & 10 Soldi coins, 1809 and 1811, from Italy, the Kingdom of Napoleon.

They found one American coin. It was a large half dollar dated 1812 and two 22 karat gold Spanish Escudos with dates of 1757 and 1792. Eight old coins had strange writing on them. Through research on the computer, Judy and Haley learned three were from India and five with square holes were from China.

"Well," said Judy, "it appears that Simon, Walter's old shipmate, traveled the world keeping a coin or two from each country he visited. This was probably his spending money and his life's savings. Wouldn't it be wonderful if these old coins could tell us about what life was like back when they were made and how Simon came to own them?"

Haley smiled and agreed that the coins would have fascinating tales to tell. Then she asked Judy, "Do you think the ditty bag, tools and coins could be worth anything?"

"Yes, I do," answered Judy. "They could be worth hundreds of dollars – but these artifacts are more than just money. They are part of your incredible story and a link to our lighthouse and all the people who have loved it since its construction in 1811.

"It's getting late. We don't have time to examine any more coins today. You found a real buried treasure! You will need to decide what to do with it. Now I think it would be a good idea to share your amazing story with your parents. I know you are saving money for your education beyond high school. Selling your treasure could add a significant amount to your college fund."

Haley nodded. Judy found a cardboard box so Haley could carry Simon and Walter's gift home.

– CHAPTER V –

That night after dinner, Haley began relating to her parents her experiences during the last Open House Weekend. Her mom and dad listened politely, occasionally smiling and asking questions, but when Haley brought out the box and began showing the ditty bag and all that was in it, her parents were speechless.

Finally, Bob exclaimed, "Wow, what a story, Haley. Those artifacts you and Judy found may be worth serious money. If they were displayed here as part of Scituate Light's history they would be priceless. If you sold them, I know there are things you would like to buy with the money as well as add to your college fund. It is your treasure and it will be your decision on what to do next. Let me do some research to find out the value of these things. It may take a little time. Are you in a big hurry?"

Haley shook her head.

Haley slept well that night, not only because she was tired from the work of finding the treasure, but she was at peace with the idea that just maybe the young boy who had visited the lighthouse was not simply a figment of her imagination. From that night on, Walter the boy from the past, and Walter the Herring Gull, would both always be real in Haley's heart.

The Gallaghers continued to talk about Haley's incredible story all week. Then everyone became busy with other things. One month went by before the treasure was mentioned again at the kitchen table. This time it was Haley's father who brought up the subject.

"Haley," he began, "first, I contacted Louis Bartos, a well known sailmaker, and sail historian, and expert familiar with traditional objects used by sailors before 1850. Mr. Bartos lives in Ketchikan, Alaska. Then I spoke with Fred Hicks, a rare coin expert in Boston. Together they estimated that what you found would sell for more than two thousand dollars."

Haley smiled from ear to ear and her parents waited for her to say, "Sell them quick!" but she didn't. She was silent for a few moments and then sat up even straighter in her chair to speak.

Haley began, "I have been thinking a lot about Walter's treasure, things I'd like to buy and money I need for college. I am hoping that six years from now I will be able to go to college by working as much as I can and also by applying for scholarships. I know it will not be easy for us to come up with the money but I think that it will be possible. Scituate Lighthouse has been our home for five years and I love it here. Our family is now part of the history of this lighthouse. The mysterious friend I made and the treasure I found will also become part of that history. I would love the money but I love Scituate Lighthouse more."

A few weeks later, at a formal meeting, Haley presented the ditty bag and its contents to the Scituate Historical Society. They accepted the treasure with the understanding that it would be displayed at the Scituate Historical Society Museum and at the Scituate Lighthouse on visiting days.

A young reporter from a local newspaper was in the audience. Immediately after the meeting adjourned, he asked Haley's parents and Haley for an interview.

A few days later, Haley told her story to the reporter, and her parents added their part. The reporter interviewed many of the people on Cedar Point that Haley had mentioned including Judy Wainwright, David Ball, Mark Walkins, the Martins, the Kincaids and many other residents who knew the Scituate Lightkeeper's family. He took pictures of all the items Haley and Judy had found and promised the story would appear in the paper in two weeks.

As promised, much to the family's surprise, Haley's picture and the treasure appeared on the front page of the local paper along with a long article relating Haley's tale of her strange meeting with a young boy at the lighthouse and her hunt for the treasure he had promised to her. The newspaper article also mentioned that Haley had given up a substantial amount of money by not selling her treasure and instead giving it to the Scituate Historical Society. Everyone who read the story was fascinated by the tale and impressed by Haley's generous gesture.

Many thousands of readers saw the local news story and soon the larger Boston newspapers wanted to write articles about Haley as well. Some people thought it could not have happened exactly as Haley described and others believed that anything is possible. Everyone agreed that Haley was a special young woman.

After the publicity nothing much changed in Haley's life – for several days. At school she received some good-natured kidding about her mysterious friend Walter, yet many kids and teachers wanted to hear the story from her own lips.

The Scituate Coastal Times

VOL. LVII No. 19,325   SATURDAY, JUNE 1ST, 2013   ONE DOLLAR

Scituate Lightkeeper's Daughter Finds Two Hundred Year-Old Treasure!

Haley Gallagher recently surprised everyone who lives in the town of Scituate by displaying a 200 hundred year-old treasure she found near the Scituate Lighthouse. She lives with her parents Bob and Julie Gallagher who are the light keepers of Scituate Light. Built in 1811 the lighthouse is located at the tip of the Cedar Point peninsula.

Haley's amazing tale is one of mystery. During an unusual pea soup fog Open House at the lighthouse in August last year, one of the visitors was a young boy wearing the clothes of a seaman from the 1800s. He asked Haley questions regarding the famous sea battle that took place a few miles from the Scituate Lighthouse between the USS Chesapeake and the HMS Shannon in June of 1814.

As the strange boy bid Haley "Good-bye" he offered her a gift – a cryptic clue to finding a nearby treasure and then he disappeared in the fog. Although Haley did not take his words seriously she decided to ask neighbors on Cedar Point about the boy who gave his name as Walter Eldridge. Most Cedar Point residents had no knowledge of someone named Walter but two neighbors helped Haley interpret Walter's clues which led to the discovery of the treasure – a sailor's ditty bag containing an old knife, sailor's needles, a bench hook and a hemp pouch containing many rare old coins.

The treasure has been valued at over two thousand dollars.

According to Haley, she and her parents love living at Scituate Lighthouse. Although Haley is saving for college she felt the right thing to would be to donate her discovery to the Scituate Historical Society. Haley's tale and treasure is now part of the history of Scituate's famous lighthouse.

What's your humor style?

In today's personality stakes, nothing is more highly valued than a sense of humor. We seek it out in others and are proud to claim it in ourselves, perhaps even more than good looks or intelligence. If someone has a great sense of humor, we reason, it means that they are happy, socially confident and have a healthy perspective on life. This attitude would have surprised the ancient Greeks, who believed humor to be essentially aggressive. And in fact, our admiration for the comedically gifted is relatively new, and not very well-founded, says Rod Martin, a psychologist at the University of Western Ontario who studies the way people use humor. Being funny isn't necessarily an indicator of good social skills and well-being, his research has shown—it may just as likely be a sign of personality flaws.

He has found that humor is a double-edged sword. It can forge better relationships and help you cope with life, or it can be corrosive, eating away at self-esteem and antagonizing others. «It's a form of communication, like speech, and we all use it differently,» says Martin. We use bonding humor to enhance our social connections—but we also may wield it as a way of excluding or rejecting an outsider. Likewise, put-down humor can at times be an adaptive, healthy response: Employees suffering under a vindictive boss will often make the office more bearable by secretly ridiculing their tyrant. Though humor is essentially social, how you use it says a lot about your sense of self. Those who use self-deflating humor, making fun of themselves for the enjoyment of others, tend to maintain that hostility toward themselves even when alone.

▶ Page 3

INSIDE

Business..................B7-12
Classifieds..............E6-10
Comics....................E3
Crossword.................D9
Editorials................A2-3
Entertainment.............D1-4
Escapes...................C9-15
Horoscope.................D5
Lotteries.................D6
Movie Listings...........E1-5
National..................B1-5
Obituaries................E11
Opinion...................B6
Sports....................C1-8
Stocks....................B14-15
Television................D11-15
Weddings..................D7
Weather...................A3
World News................A4-12

Haley Gallagher surrounded by some of the coins found in Walter's two hundred year old ditty bag

STOCK EXCHANGE   DOW JONES △ 300.74 +0.36   FTSE100 △ 6524.12 +25.54   CAC 40 △ 6070.30 +24.21   D59323E5072

On the fourth day after the first newspaper article appeared, Haley returned home from school to find twelve letters addressed to her. She couldn't imagine why anyone would write to her. She briefly sat at the kitchen table looking at the envelopes. She noticed that most of the letters were from people who lived in Scituate or nearby towns but two were from Boston.

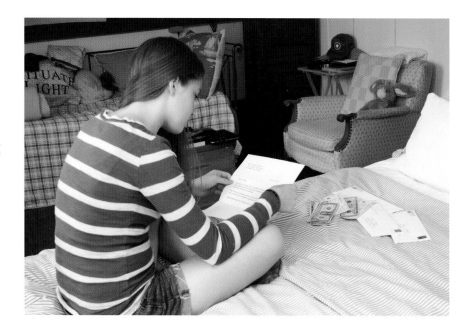

Haley took the letters to her room and began to open them. Some letters had notes thanking her for her generosity and gift to the town of Scituate. Many of those letters included cash or checks for her. Several of the letters were from local restaurants that invited Haley and her family to come for a complimentary meal, and a few were from clothing and department stores with notes of thanks and gift certificates.

After opening the last letter, Haley was stunned. She stared at all of the wonderful cards, money and gifts she held in her hands. She did not know then that the twelve letters she had just opened were to be the first of hundreds she would receive over the next few months. Every letter would convey the writer's appreciation for Haley's selflessness and most would contain a gift of some type.

Months later the final letter reached Haley and by that time the monetary value of Walter Eldridge's wee treasure had been surpassed many times over and her college fund had grown tremendously.

Haley's story had deeply touched the hearts of hundreds of people and she in turn had been touched by their overwhelming generous responses. Although Haley did not realize it at the time, her story would be repeated whenever anyone spoke of the history of the Scituate Lighthouse. Every storyteller would include the incredible tale of the Lightkeeper's Daughter and her love for Scituate Light.

PHOTO, ILLUSTRATION AND CONTRIBUTER CREDITS

Doug Andersen
doug@andersenillustration.com
pages: 3, 9, 17, 25, 31, 35 and 41 illustrations

Arial Only Gallery
Joseph R. Melanson
www.skypic.com
pages: inside front cover photo

Matthew S. Appleby, Scituate, MA
inside back cover and candid photos

Dave Ball, Scituate, MA

Louie and Jean Bartos, Ketchikan, AK
Artifact Replicas
pages: 1, 34, 37 and 39

Morgan Cole, student, Scituate, MA

Jack Costello, Plymouth, MA
www.flickr.com/photos/jjc3
page: 14 and candid photos

Georges Jacques Denton
Formerly of Scituate, MA
page: 26 reprint

Bob Gallagher, Scituate, MA
pages: 4, 5, 6 and candid photos

Haley Gallagher, student, Scituate, MA

Julie Gallagher, Scituate, MA
pages: 1, 15, 18, 21, 23, 38, 44 and candid photos

Marcia Ludlow, East Falmouth, MA

Linda Martin, Scituate, MA
pages: 10, 11, 13, 19, 27, 32, 46 and candid photos

National Maritime Museum
Greenwich, London
Object #PAH8127
The Brilliant Achievement of the *Shannon*…
in boarding and capturing the United States
Frigate *Chesapeake* off Boston June 1st 1813
in Fifteen Minutes
Aquatint by W. Elmes
http://collections.rmg.co.uk/collections/
objects/148074.html
page: 12 reproduction

"I must tell thee… Haley's wee treasure can be seen at the Scituate Historical Society Museum and on Open House Days at the Scituate Lighthouse."

Naval Historical Center
Department of the Navy
Photo #80-G-K-17587
Captain James Lawrence, USN (1781-1813)
Portrait in oil, by J. Herring
http://www.history.navy.mil/photos/images/
k16000/k17587.jpg
and
Photo #NH 65811-KN
Engagement between USS *Chesapeake*
and HMS *Shannon*, 1 June, 1813
Colored lithograph by M. Dubourg
http://www.history.navy.mil/photos/images/
h65000/h65811k.jpg
page: 12 reproductions

Mary Sellner Orr East Falmouth, MA
Pages: 38, 39 and 40 photos

Scituate Historical Society, Scituate, MA

Howard Simpson, Sterling, MA
Cover Photo

Allison Startzell, Scituate, MA
candid photos

Hayden Startzell, student, Scituate, MA

Brian Stewart, Scituate, MA
www.stewiephotos.blogspot.com
pages: 16, 45, candid and Back Cover photos

Judy Wainwright, Scituate, MA
candid photos

Richard Wainwright, Scituate, MA
pages: 2, 28, 29, 30, 33, 34, 37, 39, 41
and candid photos

CEDAR POINT CANDID PHOTOS

LIGHTHOUSE
PARK

SCITUATE BEACH ASSOCIATION
PROUDLY PRESENTS
LABOR DAY PARADE
THANK YOU FOR YOUR SUPPORT!

1636   1976

OLD SCITUATE
LIGHTHOUSE

DURING THE YEAR 1810 THE U.S.
CONGRESS VOTED 4000 TO BUILD A
LIGHTHOUSE AT SCITUATE HARBOR.
DURING THE WAR OF 1812, ABIGAIL AND
REBECCA BATES YOUNG DAUGHTERS OF
THE LIGHTHOUSE KEEPER PREVENTED
A BRITISH NAVAL FORCE FROM SACKING
THE TOWN BY PLAYING A FIFE AND
BEATING A DRUM. THEY HAVE GONE
DOWN IN HISTORY AS "THE ARMY OF
TWO" AND THEIR COURAGEOUS ACT
HAS BEEN RECORDED IN MANY
TEXTBOOKS AND STORY BOOKS.

SCITUATE HISTORICAL SOCIETY

DONT GIVE
THE SHIP

OLD SCITUATE LIGHTHOUSE